DISNEY'S
THE LITTLE MERMAID

First American Edition. Copyright © 1993
The Walt Disney Company. All rights
reserved under international copyright
conventions. Published in the United States
by Grolier Enterprises Inc., Danbury,
Connecticut. Originally published in
Denmark as Den Lille Havfrue by
Gutenberghus Gruppen, Copenhagen,
in 1990. ISBN: 0-7172-8319-4

Manufactured in the United States.

P   6 7 8 9

GROLIER
BOOK CLUB EDITION

Far beneath the ocean waves, in the land of the merpeople, lived a lovely young mermaid named Ariel. Her home was an undersea palace. Although it was quite magnificent, she hardly ever spent time there. She preferred to go exploring with her little friend Flounder, the fish.

Ariel loved to collect objects from the world above the sea. She and Flounder would swim in and out of sunken ships, picking up whatever caught the Little Mermaid's fancy.

Ariel's father, King Triton, ruled the undersea
kingdom. He was very proud of Ariel's many
gifts, especially her beautiful singing voice. He
had arranged to give a special concert to show his
daughter's wonderful talent to all the merfolk.

Ariel's sisters sang to begin the concert. Then they sang a special song to introduce Ariel.

But Ariel wasn't there!

Triton was not pleased. How could Ariel have forgotten to show up for her own debut?

As usual, Ariel was off exploring. She had found a sunken ship to play in and had forgotten all about the concert. By the time she returned home, the guests had left. Triton was so angry that he ordered Sebastian, a crab who was his court composer, to follow Ariel and to keep her out of trouble.

Later that day, Ariel slipped away again, with
Sebastian following close behind. She hadn't gone
far when a huge shadow darkened the waters
above.

"It's a ship!" she gasped with delight.

Ariel swam to the surface to get a closer look.
There were humans on board! One of them
was very handsome. Ariel heard the others call
him Prince Eric.

But as Ariel watched, a sudden storm took
them all by surprise. To her horror, the ship began
to sink. Most of the people on board were able to
climb safely into a lifeboat. But the handsome
young prince was hit by a falling spar and
thrown into the churning water.

Ariel knew that humans could not live under
the sea. She had to save the unconscious prince.
There was no time to lose!

She darted through the waves toward the
prince, as her friend, Scuttle, watched anxiously.

Using all her strength, Ariel dragged the
young prince to shore. Scuttle was waiting for
them. The silly bird put his ear close to Eric's
boot!

"Sorry, Ariel, I can't make out a heartbeat,"
said Scuttle.

Ariel placed her head on the prince's chest.
"Oh, he is breathing, Scuttle!" she cried.

She was so happy that she began to sing to the
prince. At the sound of Ariel's lovely voice, Eric's
eyelids began to flutter.

"He's going to be all right," Ariel said
gratefully. "Now I'd better get back before Father
finds out I've left."

When the prince opened his eyes, all he saw
was his faithful dog, Max, running toward him.

Ariel returned home, but she couldn't forget the human prince. As she sat thinking about him, two evil eels named Flotsam and Jetsam watched her with their cunning eyes.

"Come with us," they coaxed sweetly. "We know someone who can help you."

Ariel followed the slippery eels. Before she knew it, she was inside the deep, dark cave of Ursula, the Sea Witch!

Ursula knew how much Ariel missed Eric. She told the young mermaid that she could help her visit him — for a price!

"I will make you human so you can visit your young man," Ursula said. "But you must get him to fall in love and kiss you before the sun sets on the third day. If you fail, you will turn back into a mermaid and return to the sea as my slave!"

Then Ursula laughed wickedly. "Oh, and one other thing. You must leave your voice with me!"

Poor Ariel! She would have done anything to see the young prince again. So she signed the agreement! Then the evil witch locked Ariel's beautiful voice inside a magic seashell that she wore around her neck.

AGREEMENT BETWEEN URSULA AND ARIEL

Flounder and Sebastian watched in amazement as Ursula's magic powers changed Ariel into a human girl. Suddenly Ariel could no longer live underwater. Luckily, her two friends rushed her up to the surface so she could breathe.

Ursula cackled with glee. She intended to make sure Ariel did not get her kiss!

Once Ariel was safe on the beach, Scuttle said, "There's something different about you, Ariel. I just can't put my foot on it."

Ariel showed him her two legs. She wanted to tell Scuttle about what had happened to her. But since Ursula had taken her voice, Sebastian had to explain.

When Ariel tried to stand, she found that balancing on her new legs was harder than it looked. "You can do it," said Scuttle. "Just watch me."

Sebastian shook his head in disbelief. "How am I going to tell the king about this?" he wondered.

Meanwhile, Eric had not forgotten about the girl who had saved his life. Although he hadn't seen her, he had fallen in love with her wonderful voice. Eric would have given his entire kingdom to find her! Then, as he was walking with Max, he saw Ariel on the beach.

"Have we met before?" Eric asked, his heart skipping a beat. But his hopes were soon dashed when he found that Ariel could not speak. *She can't be the one,* he thought.

Still, the prince felt sorry for Ariel, so he
brought her to his castle. His servants fed her
and gave her pretty clothes to wear.

The next day, the prince took Ariel for a coach ride through his kingdom. "She's so lovely," Eric said to himself. "If only she were the girl I've been searching for!"

The next day, the prince took Ariel for a boat ride.

There isn't much time, thought Ariel. *If he doesn't kiss me soon, I will become Ursula's slave.*

Although Ariel didn't know it, the prince was falling in love and was just about to kiss her.

But Flotsam and Jetsam
had been watching them.
They tipped the boat over
and sent the young couple
tumbling into the water
before Ariel could get
her kiss!

Ursula had been watching the couple in her magic bubble. She decided to trick Eric so Ariel would never get her kiss. The witch transformed herself into a beautiful girl.

With Ariel's voice locked inside the seashell necklace, Ursula would sound just like Eric's true love!

The following day, as Ursula walked along the beach, the sound of Ariel's beautiful voice filled the air. Eric could hardly believe his ears! The girl who had saved his life had finally come back to him!

Quickly, the Sea Witch put a spell on Eric, and he decided to marry her right away.

Ursula's nasty trick had worked. She and Eric
were to be married on his ship that very day!

In her cabin, Ursula laughed as she looked at
her true reflection in the mirror. Luckily, Scuttle
saw Ursula's real reflection, too.

Scuttle and Flounder rushed off to find Ariel
and tell her all about the Sea Witch's latest trick.
"Don't worry, Ariel. We'll help you!" said Scuttle,
as Flounder pulled her out to the ship. Then
Scuttle flew to the ship.

With the help of sea lions, pelicans, and other
birds, Scuttle stopped the wedding. As Ariel
climbed over the railing, the birds tore at

Ursula's clothing and pulled her hair. The seashell fell from Ursula's neck. When it broke,
Ariel's voice returned to her instantly. Ariel
called out to warn the prince.

Then Eric knew he had been tricked. But time
had run out. The sun had started to set, and Ariel
was already turning back into a mermaid.

"You belong to me now!" gloated Ursula, who
had turned back into her mean, ugly self. She
grabbed Ariel and slithered into the sea.

But Eric was not about to let Ariel slip away
this time! Grabbing a harpoon, he dived into the
sea and hurled it at the Sea Witch!

That made Ursula angrier than ever! She
transformed herself into a huge monster and
tried to crush poor Ariel and the prince with
her black tentacles.

Eric clutched the Little Mermaid to him,
trying to protect her from the witch's fury.

Eric knew he had to do something, and fast!
Climbing aboard a ship that Ursula's angry
thrashing had raised from the bottom of the sea,
he grabbed the wheel. He aimed the ship's prow
at Ursula and sailed full speed ahead! As the
boat struck the witch, she let out a terrible
scream. Then she was gone forever!

Everyone was glad the Sea
Witch was gone, but Ariel was
still unhappy. Even Triton
could see that his daughter
was truly in love. So, using
his magic powers, he granted
Ariel her dearest wish — he
made her human again.

Triton watched as Eric and Ariel walked toward the castle.

"I'm going to miss her," King Triton said to Sebastian, "but I know they'll be happy."

Soon after that, Eric and Ariel were married in a splendid shipboard wedding with all the merpeople looking on. And just as King Triton had predicted, they lived happily ever after!